Decorate this cute cake display. Make the frosting on the cupcakes different flavors, and add your own pretty design to the tablecloth.

Yum!

Cookies, cups, and saucers—it's time for tea!

Add your own cookie or teacup to the china plate.

Color in the tasty treats in this pretty bakery window.
Add your favorite cookies and cakes to the empty plates.

Yum! Make these fabulous fruits look good enough to eat.

Princess Poppy is on her way to the Toadstool Ball! Draw a flowery design on her dress.

Garlands and balloons—it's time
for a princess party!

Nick the knight is guarding the castle.
Give him shiny blue armor and decorate
the castle with your favorite colors.

Here is Princess Snowflake!
Draw a frosty pattern on her dress.

Sparkling jewels and glittering gold!
Make these tiaras and crowns fit
for any princess.

Draw in lots of flowers growing in the castle's
garden to make it a perfect princess home.

Here are two little unicorns, Misty and Rainbow.
Use your colors to complete this magical picture.

Dot is on her way to meet her fairy friends!
Draw a dainty design on her dress.

Fairies and unicorns!
Color in this enchanted scene.

Pins, buttons, and ribbons—it's time to sew!
Color in these pretty sewing things.

Add your own designs to these fancy hats!

Draw your own patterns onto these pretty tops and dresses.

Jewels, rings, and sparkling things! Color in these gems and trinkets.

Pizza and pajamas—
let's have a sleepover!
Draw in some more snacks for
Livvy and Libby to eat.

Fill this pretty pattern with your favorite colors.

Draw your own design onto Pippa the pop star's dress.

Let's make music! Color this violin, however you like!

Add your own design to Bella the ballerina's tutu.
Which colors will you use?

Here is Bella's costume for Cinderella.
Make her outfit pretty enough for a princess!

Ella is at the masquerade ball.
Decorate her gown and mask to complete her outfit.

Rosie the florist is busy in her flower shop.
Draw in lots of flowers for her to sell.

Lots of lazy daisies! Color in this lovely flower chain.

Raindrops and sunbeams!

Color in this beautiful rainbow.

Fluttering butterflies!
Give these beautiful butterflies
brightly colored wings.

Who is singing sweetly in the tree? Color in this family of bluebirds.

Tweet, tweet!

Tweet, tweet!

Two little snails having fun among the flowers. Color in this garden scene.

Starlight and campfires! Complete this campsite scene.

Hoot! Hoot! Add your own wise owl to the branch.

There are lots of visitors at the puppy park today! Draw in your own puppy pal and color in the scene.

Woof! Woof!

Hop, hop, hop!
Add your own little cottontail friend
to the bunny meadow.

Meow!

Purr!

Three furry bundles! Color in these cute kittens.

Here are three little ponies—
Chestnut, Plum, and Daisy.
Color in their pretty pony paddock.

What's going on down at the farm? Color in this busy barnyard scene.

Moo!

Baa!

Oink, oink!

Anna the vet is looking after an injured puppy.
Can you draw a bandage on his leg?

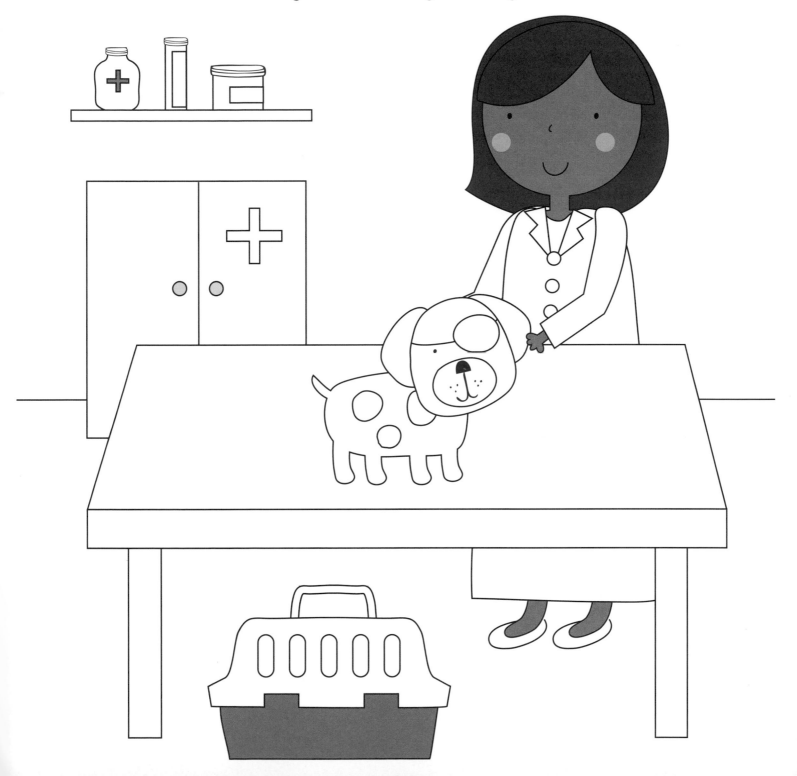

Whiskers the cat has hurt his paw!
Draw in some cat toys and treats to help him feel better.

Let's go to the zoo!
Which animals can you see?

ZOO

Sweet, little ears and big, round eyes!
Color in these cute panda cubs.

This rainforest is full of tropical plants and animals.
Fill it up with lots of bright colors!

Evie the explorer has spotted two monkeys playing.
Color in this safari scene.

Who's that hiding in the palm tree?
Add another sneaky creature to this jungle picture.

Color in these cute ocean creatures.

Let's go to the beach!
Draw in some friends having
fun by the sea.

Starfish and seashells! Color in these pretty seashore things.

Here is Milly the mermaid! Draw a pretty pattern on her tail.